The Fall Gathering

By Rita Kohn

Illustrated by Winifred Barnum-Newman

The Woodland Adventures series
is dedicated to all The Woodland People
who persevere despite hardships, inhumanity, and hostility.
Their spirit, like the Eagle, soars.
Their integrity, like the Turtle, persists.

This book is dedicated to
Carra, Jason, and Joel,
who have joined the sharing
time of an extended family.

Special thanks to:
Wap Shing, spiritual Leader of the Miami of Indiana,
and to my Consultants
Curtis Zunigha - Lenape (Delaware) and Isleta Pueblo,
James Rementer and Michael Pace - Delawares of Eastern Oklahoma,
Brenda Ballew - Pokagon Potawatomi,
and Beth Kohn - Early Childhood Specialist;
and to my Teachers
Emma Donaldson and Billie Smith - Elders, Loyal Band Shawnee

Kohn, Rita T.
    The fall gathering / by Rita Kohn; Illustrated by Winifred Barnum-Newman.
    p. cm. - (Woodland adventures)

    ISBN 0-516-05202-0

    1. Indians of North America -- Great Lakes Region -- Social life and
customs -- Juvenile literature. 2. Woodland Indians -- Social life and
customs -- Juvenile literature. 3. Harvest festivals -- Great Lakes
Region -- Juvenile literature. [1. Woodland Indians--Social life and
customs. 2. Indians of North America -- Great Lakes Region -- Social
life and customs. 3. Counting. 4. Harvest Festivals. 5. Autumn.]
I. Barnum-Newman, Winifred, ill. II. Title. III. Series.
E78.G7K65 1995
394.2 ' 64 '089973 -- dc20   94-38378
                                                          CIP
                                                          AC

Project Editor: Alice Flanagan
Design and Electronic Production:
    PCI Design Group, San Antonio, Texas
Engraver: Liberty Photoengravers
Printer: Lake Book Manufacturing, Inc.

1 2 3 4 5 6 7 8 9 R 04 03 02 01 00 99 98 97 96 95

The Purpose of This Book

The Fall Gathering, one of four books
having a SEASONAL theme in the
Woodland Adventures series, is a picture book
for preschool and primary grades based on learning
the concept of QUANTITY, such as
how much and how many.

The story takes place in the fall in a
woodland region along the Great Lakes of
North America, the traditional homeland for more
than twenty NATIVE AMERICAN nations.
It focuses on The Woodland People's annual
tradition of gathering to share in and give thanks
for a plentiful harvest. By counting how much is
brought to share at the harvest and how many
people are needed to carry out a particular task,
children strengthen their counting skills
as well as learn the significance
of sharing and cooperation.

The harvest
is in.

Just as the white and yellow sun peeks over the horizon, everyone arrives at the gathering place.

They have come to share the harvest.

6

They bring

big cooking pot
and some meat,

8

2

large
fire logs,

9

3

choices
of
nuts,

10

4

types
of
squash,

11

5

kinds

of

beans,

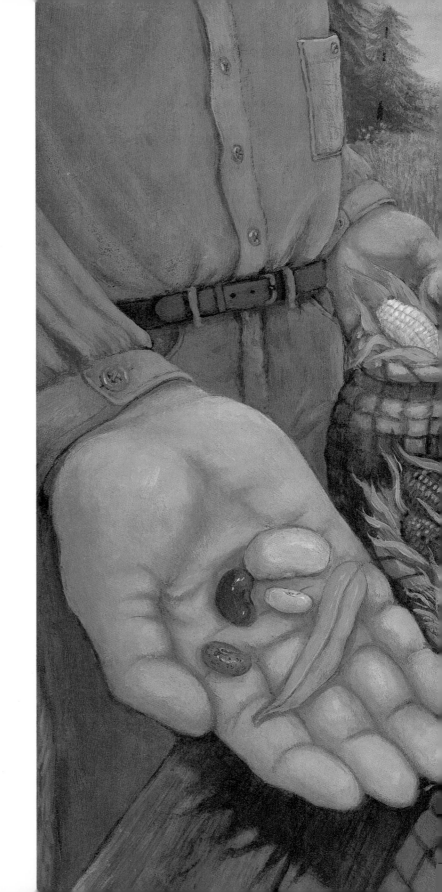

6

baskets

with

corn,

13

7

varieties
of root
vegetables,

8

loads
of
berries,

9

trays of
fry
bread,

16

10

jugs
of fruit
drink.

Some
people cook.

Some people
set tables.

21

At the end
of the day,
all that is left
is the empty pot,
baskets,
and trays.

25

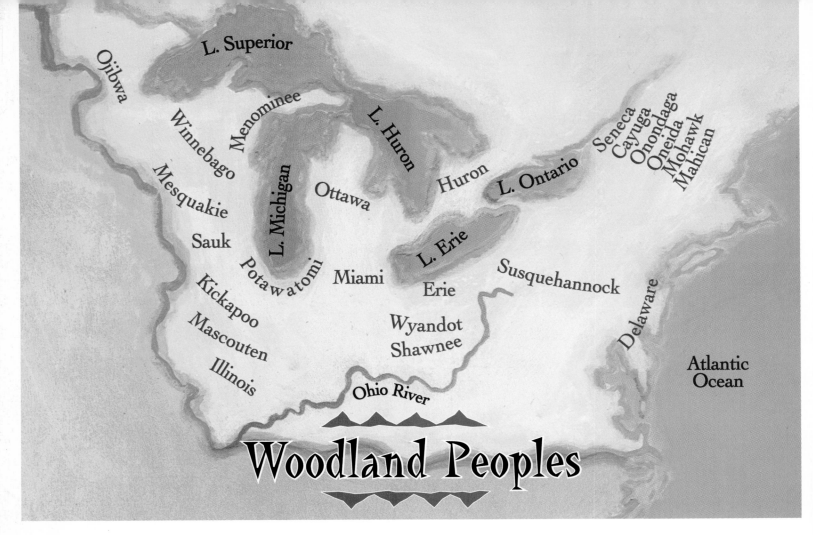

Ojibwa

L. Superior

Menominee

Winnebago

L. Huron

Mesquakie

L. Michigan

Ottawa

Huron

L. Ontario

Seneca
Cayuga
Onondaga
Oneida
Mohawk
Mahican

Sauk

Potawatomi

Miami

L. Erie

Susquehannock

Kickapoo

Erie

Delaware

Mascouten

Wyandot
Shawnee

Atlantic
Ocean

Illinois

Ohio River

Woodland Peoples

The traditional homeland of the People of the Great Lakes woodland has many rivers and lakes and, originally, was filled with forests and grasslands. Here lived the Five Nations of the League of the Iroquois -- the Mohawk, Oneida, Onondaga, Cayuga, and Seneca; and the individual Nations including the Huron, Wyandot, Ottawa, Ojibwa (commonly called Chippewa), Menominee, Dakota, Mesquakie (commonly called Fox), Sauk, Winnebago, Potawatomi, Kickapoo, Mascouten, Miami, and Shawnee.

When the Atlantic Ocean coastal region was settled by Europeans, many Indians who lived there moved to the Great Lakes region. They include the Mahican, Munsi, Lenape (commonly called Delaware), Nanticoke, Piscataway, and Osage.

British treaties giving native peoples the right to live peacefully for all time in the Great Lakes region were not honored by the government of the United States of America. By 1840, land occupied by native people living closest to the Ohio River was taken away.

The Fall Gathering

Each year, The Woodland People gather to share in and give thanks for a bountiful harvest. All who are in need are looked after so no one will go hungry during the cold winter ahead. Originally, each tribe relied on what grew best in its area or what was most easily gathered or hunted. In the northern Great Lakes region, it was fish and wild rice. Closest to the Ohio River, it was corn, beans, and squash. Everyone gathered berries and nuts and in the early spring left their home-base villages to set up temporary villages in maple groves for the annual sugarmaking event. Today, many kinds of grains, vegetables, fruits, meats, and condiments are available to everyone.

At the gathering, many tribes continue their traditional ways and pass on their heritage of giving thanks, showing respect, and sharing. Elders are served first, young people go last. Blessings acknowledge the unity of all living things with the creator. From this traditional gathering probably came the custom of "Thanksgiving Dinner," which may have begun in 1621 between Eastern Woodland Indians and Europeans who began the Massachusetts Bay Colony, and which continues today as part of our American cultural tradition.

About the Author

Rita Kohn grew up in the Catskill Mountains, went to college in Buffalo, New York, and now calls both Illinois and Indiana home. All these places are part of the ancestral territory of the Woodland People. A lifelong love of the land and the People whose spirit continues to give energy to these mountains, valleys, streams, lakes, and fields leads her to listen, watch, and learn. Her book is one way of continuing the circle of life.

About the Illustrator

Winifred Barnum-Newman is an award-winning artist, author, and illustrator who maintains a keen interest in Native American culture. Her husband of thirty-two years, an artist and advertising executive, is part Cherokee and often her consultant on projects pertaining to Native Americans.

Barnum-Newman, who is the mother of two daughters, brings to her work a love of children and a sensitivity for the culture she is representing. Her work encompasses sculpture, painting, graphics, writing, and illustrating. Born in Kansas City, Missouri, she now makes her home in Texas.